I0763434

Copyright © 2018 by Lucinda Whitney
Published by Lange House Press
Cover design ©2019 Lange House Press
ISBN-13: 978-1-987431-23-0

All rights reserved. This book is a work of fiction. Names, characters, places, and incidents are either a product of the author's imagination or are used fictitiously. Any resemblance to actual events, locales, or persons, living or dead, is entirely coincidental. No part of this book can be reproduced in any form or by electronic or mechanical means, including information storage and retrieval systems, without the express written permission of the author.

OTHER BOOKS BY LUCINDA WHITNEY

Royal Secrets

Serving The Prince

Rescuing The Prince

Protecting The Princess

Romano Family

Hold Me At Twilight

Meet Me At Sunrise

Love Me At Sunset

Keep Me At Christmas

Kiss Me At Midnight

Marry Me At Dawn

A Love Story From Portugal

The Secret Life of Daydreams

One Small Chance

LUCINDA WHITNEY

Chapter One

Julie Winters set the platter of fries in front of the two women. “Enjoy!”

Across the common entrance and into the restaurant, the new guys were back, the ones who’d first showed up last week. They trailed the hostess who sat them at one of the VIP tables. As with everyone else who frequented the restaurant of the Blue Mountain Country Club and Lodge in Silver Springs, Colorado, they were most likely celebrities of some kind, but she didn’t recognize them. The rumor mill said they were from Europe, and, according to Ashlyn, their accents sounded like it.

She retrieved an order of beer from Peter and had it sitting on the counter when Ashlyn approached to pick up the glasses.

“They’re back. Without entourage,” Ashlyn said as she filled her tray, keeping her eyes on the drinks.

"Who's back?" Julie pulled out a lemon and cut it in wedges. Ashlyn would call her bluff, but Julie didn't want to admit she'd noticed the men had come alone today.

Ashlyn raised an eyebrow, but didn't comment. "They're asking for two Manhattans."

"On it," Julie replied. She got Peter's attention and relayed the order to him.

Julie served late dinners and snacks at the bar, and didn't have the license to serve cocktails. Ashlyn worked at the restaurant waitressing the tables. They'd met two years prior and had become friends before deciding to share an apartment. Most of the time, their schedules at the lodge restaurant didn't coincide.

Wednesday nights were not as busy as the weekend, but tonight was more crowded than the usual midweek day. As Julie didn't have the time to spend on the internet keeping up with current events, she briefly wondered if there was a reason that had attracted more guests on this night.

"I knew they wouldn't stay by themselves for too long," Ashlyn said, settling the round tray on the polished counter.

Julie raised her head and glanced at the table. True enough, three model-looking women had joined the European men.

Julie pulled out clean glasses. "Not surprised," she said, under her breath.

Ashlyn leaned against the bar while she waited for the next round of cocktails. "I'd say. One of them looks like the actor who plays Tarzan and the other one like the new Superman."

The comparison was spot-on—both tall, in their mid-twenties, one blond and the other one dark haired with a cleft chin, dressed as if they'd just stepped off an Italian fashion runway. She couldn't tell the color of their eyes from this far. The dark-haired guy had the kind of smile that could make a woman forget her name, but the blond one's expression seemed more genuine. What was his name?

The thought stopped her and Julie purposefully turned to the shelves behind the bar. How many times had she looked their way tonight? Pathetic. She was doing the same as all the other women who fawned over good-looking men. These men would never notice her anyway—they were surrounded by beauty-queens, the kind with perfectly manicured hands, salon-paid highlights, and plastic-surgery curves.

Julie was the regular girl-next-door, the one nobody gave a second look. Brown hair, brown eyes, average height. She actually didn't mind the lack of attention. It helped her concentrate on what was important in her life right now, like graduating in one year. Until then, she was grateful this job helped her pay the bills, even if sometimes the distractions of the male variety proved hard to ignore.

Ten minutes later, when Julie had a moment to look up, the dark-haired guy sat with two girls, but there was no sign of the blond one. She straightened and glanced at the table again, a slower gaze this time since Mr. Tarzan wasn't there to catch her watching him. A little twinge of something she didn't want to think about pricked in her chest, and she quickly dismissed it. Why was she even thinking about a man who didn't know she existed? She hadn't served him and he hadn't looked her way. End of story.

"Julie," Peter said with a nod towards the end of the bar.

She'd been so distracted, she'd hardly noticed the man sitting there.

He wore a light salmon shirt, the sleeves rolled up to his elbows, with his arms leaning effortlessly on the polished wood, and an empty glass sitting on the round ceramic coaster. She hesitated a moment as she recognized the blond man from the table. It was too late to ask someone else to take his order.

She ran her palms down the side of her black slacks. "What can I do for you?" She gave him the professional smile, the one she used with the guests at the lodge.

He straightened in his seat which brought him to eye level with her. His eyes were gray, the pupil ringed with light flecks of gold and blue, lending a warm tone to what should have been a cold color. For a moment, she stared at him, unable to draw away from the pull of his gaze.

Slowly, his eyes crinkled at the corners and a smile lit his face. "It's Julie, right?"

She frowned. "How do—?"

He gestured to the name tag pinned to her shirt. "I saw you earlier."

He'd noticed her? Her cheeks flamed. Maybe all the covert looks she'd sent his way hadn't been as stealthy as she'd thought. Add a new one to her file of embarrassing situations.

She nodded. "Can I get a refill on your Manhattan?"

"Do you always remember everyone's drinks?" The corner of his mouth pulled up in a teasing manner.

He had a subtle European accent. Not from Durham, and definitely not from Galia or Aragonia. She filed her curious thought away. It really didn't matter where he was from. He was only a guest who'd read her name tag.

Julie shrugged. "It comes with the job."

As she reached for the empty glass, he picked it up at the same time. His fingers brushed lightly against hers and she stilled at the unexpected contact, a current of static quickening her pulse. The glass lay suspended between them.

After an instant, he released it. "Henry's the one who likes Manhattans. Do you have any Krone beer?"

"We do," she replied. "I'll be right back."

She walked to the refrigerated section, glad for the extra seconds to compose herself from her surprise reaction to his touch. What was wrong with her tonight? He was just a man. An attractive one with a foreign accent, but a man just the same. She should be used to it by now, after working here for two years. The lodge catered to the exclusive crowd, and she'd seen plenty of rich and famous guys who dressed like GQ models and elegant businessmen, among the actors, singers, and athletes who made the guest list. They knew they could come here without being followed by paparazzi or fans sneaking pictures. That's what their money paid for.

Then why was she reacting to this one man? What made him special that her heart skipped a beat when he turned that smile on her? She didn't even particularly like blond guys, not after dating Jared the Jerk. But the guy at the end of the bar had the warmest gray eyes, kind eyes, which apparently she was partial to.

"Here you go." She placed a tall glass and the bottle of imported beer in front of him, careful to remove her fingers before he reached for it.

"Max." He extended his hand to her. "My name is Max."

Julie took his strong hand, the warmth of his fingers enveloping hers. Even as her mind told her to keep it brief, her heart squelched the common sense immediately.

"Nice to meet you, Max," she said.

"The pleasure is all mine, Julie." Was it her imagination or did his deep voice slow down when he said her name?

He squeezed her hand, and she returned the gesture before letting go.

"Do you mind if I stay over at this end for a while?" he asked.

Something in his expression and tone made her take notice. "No, of course not."

He glanced over his shoulder. "My friend found… better company."

She followed his eyes, to the place where his friend laughed easily with the two model girls. "Stay as long as you want," Julie told him, putting on a calm expression that contradicted her fast pulse.

If she'd been working the tables like she sometimes did, she never would have had the chance to talk to Max. Waitresses kept too busy to chat with the guests. Julie brushed the thought aside. She was not sitting at the bar with him, but across from him. She had work to do, and would do well to remember it.

After filling orders for five minutes, she gravitated toward the end of the bar, wiping the wood counter as she went, more to give her hands something to do and less to keep the polished wood unmarked.

Max was still sitting in the same spot, slowly sipping his beer, and didn't seem in any hurry to go anywhere else.

"Can I get you a refill?" she asked Max.

He shook his head. "No, thanks. We drove separately, but I might have to take Henry back to his cabin."

"You're a good friend, sacrificing your night so he can have fun." She chanced the comment, hoping he wouldn't find it too personal.

His expression relaxed. "Henry and I have been friends for quite a while. We grew up taking turns being responsible. Old habits are hard to break, especially when we're so far from home."

Did that mean sometimes Max was the one drinking too much with girls at his side? Whether it happened or not, it was none of her business.

"Is this your first time in the United States?"

"For me, yes. We started in Los Angeles, and now we're making our way back to New York through several states before going home."

"And home is where?"

A muscle in his jaw twitched. "In Europe."

He didn't want to tell her more details. Maybe she'd overstepped her position with too many questions, however friendly she sounded.

"And you?" he asked.

"Me?" Julie tried to buy some time. "What about me?"

"What is your story, Julie?"

He watched her with unmistakable interest as if he could find out who she really was without any words between them. How did he do it? How did he hold her so mesmerized with only his gray eyes and his half smile? She wanted to tell him everything—her dreams and ambitions, her fears and worries—and hoped he wouldn't judge her for what she lacked.

"Excuse me," a man's voice interrupted.

Julie stepped away from her spot in front of Max, feeling her cheeks flame again. She served the new guest, wishing Max would linger a little longer, but knowing it would probably be best if he left. She couldn't have this kind of distraction, wouldn't give in to a pair of eyes who watched her with the kind of attention she hadn't had in a long time, if ever. How could he be interested in her? For sure, she'd imagined it.

When the other man walked away, Max stood and handed her a bill. "Keep the change."

The tip was substantial, but she'd been trained to never question a guest over the matter of a gratuity. It wasn't good manners, and the owners of Blue Mountain wouldn't abide such behavior.

Once again, he made eye contact with her.

Addressing him by his name would be too intimate, but using the customary sir would mark the difference between them even more. So she left them both out. "Thank you." She added a genuine smile to emphasize her words.

Something passed in his eyes, but quickly left. "Thank you, Julie," he said before walking away.

Julie rang up his bill, forcing her eyes away from his retreating form.

Ashlyn approached with an order. "You have to tell me everything," Ashlyn said with a wink while she waited for more drinks and cocktails.

"Tell you what?"

"What did you and Mr. Tarzan talk about?" Ashlyn asked.

"There really isn't much to tell."

Ashlyn filled her tray. "Right. I could see the chemistry between you two from across the room, and you have nothing to say about it."

"You're imagining things," Julie replied. The chemistry was one-sided, borne from Julie's pathetic lack of a love life. Her lonely heart had latched on to the first guy who'd said her name in a long time. She'd always been attracted to guys with deep voices, and his did something to her. Something too delicious.

Ashlyn gave her a pointed look as she left to deliver the drinks.

Julie blew out a breath, steeling herself for Ashlyn's insistence that would come later. Her friend was curious, and sometimes too optimistic.

When a boisterous group came in, Julie looked their way.

Her heart skipped a beat—Max stood by the open door, his gaze fixed on her.

Out of nowhere, his friend popped back inside, the two blonde girls in too-short dresses hanging from each of his arms. He clapped Max on the shoulder and laughed. Max trailed after the trio, but not before casting one last look her way.

Was it reluctance she'd seen in his posture, or something completely different?

Chapter Two

"Max, you can't be serious," Henry said in a mocking tone. "The barmaid?"

"What are you talking about?" Max kept walking toward where they'd parked their cars earlier, trying to hide his irritation at Henry and the girls at his friend's side.

Why did Henry always insist on spending time with the flashiest, dimmest girls he could find?

It was all for show. Henry never drank enough to lose all control, but he liked to give the impression he did. He and Max had argued about this several times, since Max didn't agree with Henry's need to hide behind the façade of alcohol. Tonight he'd drank just enough to impair his reflexes, if not his judgment. Even though it would only take a few minutes to drive to their cabins, Max didn't want to leave anything to chance. He could jog from his own cabin and get his car in the morning.

He sent a quick text to Olsen, his security detail, and Michaels, Henry's bodyguard, before they came to the rescue. Max didn't want the extra attention.

Max waited while Henry said good-bye to the young women who'd been with him all night, amid giggles and lipstick-stained kisses.

"Give me your keys," he said to Henry after the girls left.

"Michaels can drive me," Henry replied.

"I told him I'd do it."

The drive was short and Max parked in the private driveway, then walked Henry toward his cabin without a word to his friend. Henry could take it from here.

By the time Max peeled off his clothes and lay down in his own bed, fatigue was catching up with him. But his mind had other ideas.

Julie of the big brown eyes.

Such an unexpected twist. He'd been in America for almost two months and how many women had caught his eye? None that he'd wanted to ask for a phone number. Certainly not in Hollywood or Las Vegas.

But here he was, in the outskirts of Denver, wondering how he could find out more about the young woman who'd served him Danish beer without knowing his family owned part of the brewery back home.

He'd always been partial to brunettes. Growing up in a country with so many blonde, blue-eyed women, including the ones in his family, brown eyes and dark hair appealed to him.

Julie's eyes had a warmth and depth that had taken him by surprise. The connection had been there, as if she could see him beyond his title. How many people at Blue Mountain knew the truth about him and Henry? They'd asked for discretion, as they had at the other places they'd stayed, and, so far, it seemed like they had it. Despite their keeping a low profile about their identity, word still got out sometimes. But Julie hadn't given any indication she knew he was related to the royals of Markendom. Had she recognized Henry? The royal house of Durham was more popular and Henry was fodder for the European tabloids often enough.

Max let out a long breath and scrubbed his face. This lifestyle was getting old really fast. What happened to all the plans he and Henry had made? It was time for a talk.

In the early morning, after a long jog around the golf course, Max retrieved his car from the restaurant's parking lot, had a hot shower, and walked the short distance to Henry's cabin. He found him sprawled on the king size bed, alone. At least there was that.

"Why aren't you up yet?" Max asked as he raised the blinds.

Light flooded the bedroom and Henry groaned, dragging a pillow over his head. "Blast it, Max, it's too early."

"We have an appointment with the representative from SkyLabs, remember?"

Henry took a peek from under the pillow. "You can go. I trust you."

"Yeah, I can go, but I can't represent Durham. That's your job."

Henry tossed the pillow on the floor. "No, it's Alex's job."

Alex was the crown prince of Durham and Henry's older brother. He did represent the crown, but so did Henry and Stefan, the middle brother, as well as their younger sister Victoria.

"I would rather you come to the meeting with me." It would be better for both of them to be there.

Henry didn't move from his position.

"I'm going to make you a cup of coffee," Max said. "Get in the shower."

Sometimes, dealing with Henry felt like dealing with a younger brother who needed help with everything.

The corporate office for SkyLabs was located in Denver's industrial park. Max pulled up into the guest parking and Henry followed. When they entered the lobby, the blonde receptionist at the round desk looked up, then straightened her shoulders and put on a wide smile.

Henry's interest perked up and he quickly approached. "How do you do?" He flashed a grin at the woman.

"I'm doing very fine. How are you?" She fluttered her eyelashes.

Max suppressed an eye roll. "Max Wolfe and Henry Somerset. We have an appointment with SkyLabs."

At his professional tone, the receptionist wiped her flirty grin. "Yes, sir, Mr. Wolfe."

In the elevator, Max fixed a stare at his friend and shook his head.

"What?" Henry asked, as if not knowing what Max meant. "I was just being friendly."

Max didn't comment. Henry was always friendly.

SkyLabs led the market in fiber optic internet. Max had contacted them and they'd invited him and Henry for a presentation. If they liked what they saw, they would talk to their families about the opportunity for investment. Even if his family wasn't interested, Max was considering investing on his own.

Max and Henry were greeted by two men in their early forties who took them into a luxuriously decorated conference room. No expense had been spared and it was obvious the company was trying to impress them. Max hoped the content matched his expectations.

The presentation turned out a bit longer than what Max had anticipated, and the overload of information was almost too much. Henry had lost his interest already, as he kept glancing at his phone periodically. As the lunch hour approached, Max tried to come up with a good excuse to leave, but duty and upbringing kept him from interrupting.

Just then, the intercom buzzed. "Mr. Quail, the delivery is here," the feminine voice said.

Mr. Quail, the shorter, younger man, stood from his chair. "Excellent. Just the interruption we needed." He smiled. "We arranged for a catered lunch from the Blue Mountain Restaurant, one of the few Michelin star establishments in Denver."

Mr. Kilfoyle, the other SkyLab representative, laced his fingers. "If you haven't been there, you're in for a treat."

Henry smirked, but didn't say anything. He and Max had been staying at the Blue Mountain Lodge for well over a week and had dined at the restaurant several times.

Max stood and stretched his legs. The room had an excellent view toward the downtown area of Denver with the mountains in the background. Even though it was the middle of April, plenty of snow still capped the peaks. Maybe he'd return for ski season.

A soft knock sounded at the door and someone rushed to open it.

"Where would you like me to put these?"

There was a familiar tone to the feminine voice, but Max couldn't quite place it. When he turned, a woman with brown hair stood with her back to him, removing containers from thermal bags and placing them onto a serving table. She reached into another bag and set down the plates, napkins, and silverware to the side, pulled out the drinks and glasses, and lastly proceeded to unbox and plate the food.

She turned and smiled. "Today we have a sirloin with wild rice and—"

He didn't hear the rest, fixed as he was on her face.

Her gaze went around the room, and when her brown eyes landed on him, her pleasant expression froze.

Julie.

Her hair was in a chignon instead of a pony tail, but he'd dreamt of those eyes. She wore a white button shirt and black slacks instead of the restaurant's uniform, and now that she wasn't standing behind the bar, he could better appreciate her shapely form.

Henry's attention perked up and he stood, ready

to lay on his charm, as he usually did in the presence of attractive women.

Max walked in front of Henry. "How are you, Julie?"

"I'm doing well. Thank you." She nodded at him in acknowledgment and Max nodded back.

Henry stopped. "You know each other?"

"Yes, we do." Max slipped his hands in his pockets and leveled a stare at Henry. Max was acting like a territorial jerk, but he'd had enough of Henry's carousing.

Julie turned to the other men. "I'll be back in an hour to clear up, Mr. Quail."

"That will be great. Thanks."

The lunch was delicious, but an odd sort of tension had risen between Max and Henry and the other men could sense it. They ended the meeting shortly after and Max promised he'd be in contact soon. He needed the time to research other investments in the same field.

When they arrived at the parking lot, Henry let out a low chuckle. "You could have told me that you've got something going on with the waitress. She looks familiar. Isn't she actually the barmaid?"

Max unlocked the car and opened the door. "No, I don't have anything going on with the waitress. Or anyone else, for that matter," he added.

"Then what was that macho showdown you gave me back there for?"

"Not every woman you meet is a conquest waiting for you. Have you thought about that?" This time the annoyance showed in Max's voice, and he didn't care.

Henry smirked. "I'm a friendly bloke and the ladies like me. I can't help it and I certainly won't say no." He shrugged. "But I'll back off since you're interested in her."

Max gritted his teeth and didn't reply. There was too much between him and Henry to ruin it about someone he really didn't know. He drove Henry back to his cabin and then left, needing the space away from his friend and the time to clear his head.

Was he interested in Julie?

Unlike Henry, Max didn't feel the need for constant female company. He'd dated while at university, even had a girlfriend for some time, but his status and title always seemed to be of more interest to the girls than he himself was as a man. Being the second son of the royal family wasn't something he could get away from in Markendom, and if he couldn't date a genuine woman, he rather not date at all. Or at least, he could put it off until he found someone sincere.

Chapter Three

The alarm went off and Julie grabbed the phone to silence it. On Saturdays she could sleep in past seven in the morning. No school, no work. But her body clock was too used to her weekday routine and after a few minutes of looking around her small bedroom, she rose and got in the shower.

The sewing machine sat on the floor by the coffee table, and, judging from the dress hanging from the back of the door, Ashlyn was already gone. She must have worn a different dress to the dancing studio she frequented on Saturdays. Her passion for Latin music and her fashion major combined perfectly, and Ashlyn was good at both.

For breakfast, Julie blended a plain Greek yogurt with frozen blueberries and a banana, added a spoon of ground flaxseed, and topped it with slivered almonds. She ate it, then opened the window. The air was cool, and the trees across the street hinted at spring.

Julie was ready for a change. For warmer days and green grass. For a break from school and less working hours, for more time spent outside or some place away from responsibilities and the weight of everyday life.

She sighed. Not for a while.

After washing the few dishes in the sink, she looked in the refrigerator and the cupboards and wrote down her weekly shopping list. The apartment was small and didn't take more than one hour to clean before she was ready to go to the store. Laundry would come later in the evening. When most tenants in her building were busy with Saturday night activities, Julie would take her basket of wash, and sit on a camp chair in the laundry room catching up with her required reading for her classes. Not like she had any better plans. Ashlyn had a late shift which meant she wouldn't be around to insist Julie went with her somewhere in the city.

Her phone rang just as Julie finished up cleaning the bathroom.

"Julie," Ashlyn said loudly.

Julie flinched away from her phone. "I'm right here, Ashlyn. No need to scream. What's going on?"

"An emergency. You're not on the schedule today, are you?"

"It's my day off." Ashlyn knew Julie's schedule as well as her own. "Don't scare me. What kind of emergency?"

"It's not scary, it's good." Ashlyn rushed her words. "Do you remember that guy I met at the Jitter Bug last month?"

Ashlyn went dancing every week, and the Jitter Bug was her favorite dance club.

"The salsa guy?" Julie had a vague recollection of Ashlyn going on and on about a Latin dancer.

"The samba guy, not salsa. Anyway, he asked me out, Julie. He wants to go dancing with me."

"That's great, Ashlyn. Congrats." Ashlyn had talked so much about it. "So what's the problem?"

"I'm supposed to work today." Ashlyn's voice took on a tone of pleading. "Can you please take my shift, Julie?"

Julie suppressed a groan. She still had to go shopping for the week, not to mention the laundry and her text books. But the extra hours would come in handy, and she wasn't in a position to say no to money. Whenever she got the chance, Julie sent some money home to help her mother and her two teenage brothers.

"Sure, I'll do it. Thanks for thinking of me. At what time?"

Ashlyn squealed. "You're the best, Julie. I'll make it up to you, I promise."

Julie hung up after getting the details. She ate a sandwich, then changed into her uniform, and tucked her shopping list in her purse. Maybe she'd have the time to swing by the market on the way back home from work.

The small American-made beater she'd been driving for years sat in the sun. Their rent didn't include covered parking spots, which meant Julie suffered through the seasons—scraping the snow off the windshield in the winter, and roasting in the summer, as the air conditioning hadn't worked in some time. At least today the temperature was still on the cooler side.

She turned the key in the ignition. The old car sputtered and a hint of fear rose in her throat. Not right now. Not when she'd promised Ashlyn to take her shift. She closed her eyes and said a little prayer, then turned the key again. After an initial struggle, it started and Julie let out a whoop and a loud thank-you.

In good traffic, it only took her fifteen to twenty minutes to drive to the Blue Mountain where the restaurant was located. Her apartment was closer to campus, and she usually walked, unless the weather was too bad, then she rode the bus.

As she drove past the edge of town, the car sputtered again.

"No-no-no-no," Julie said under her breath, as if pleading with the car to keep working.

The sputters increased in volume and frequency, followed by a string of pops that sounded like popcorn in the microwave. She frowned. This couldn't be good. Julie quickly pulled over to the shoulder, and just then a loud bang exploded from under the hood. She jumped in her seat and scrambled to turn off the ignition, then sat there until her heartbeat returned to normal. Why hadn't it died closer to the gas station she'd passed a few minutes before?

Julie unbuckled and pulled out her cell phone, then scrolled through the contacts list until she found the shift manager's number. David wouldn't be happy she was late. She didn't have anyone she could call for a ride, not on this side of town, and not with Ashlyn gone to the club in Denver.

The crunch of a car on the soft gravel forced her eyes from the phone screen. A car had parked right behind her and a tall man wearing sunglasses exited. Great, just what she needed. What if the guy was a creep? Julie locked the doors. She'd tell him she was making a phone call.

A knock sounded on the glass. "Is everything all right?"

Julie steeled herself and took a deep breath, then palmed her phone and turned to the window with a smile. The guy had crouched by the door and seeing him at her eye level startled her.

Her free hand landed on her chest. "Yes, yes, I'm okay," she replied a little too fast. She slowed her words and held the phone up. "See? I'm just making a call." Hopefully he wouldn't notice how much her voice trembled.

A slow smile dimpled his right cheek and he removed the sunglasses. His eyes were the color of light granite and familiar.

Max.

"Hello, Julie," he said.

His voice came muffled from the other side.

"Hi," she said.

He made the gesture for her to roll down the window, but she couldn't since the car wasn't working.

She hesitated, then unlocked the car and cracked the door open.

Max stood and stepped back, then leaned closer to her. "Did you run out of gas or something?"

"Or something. But I'm okay. No need to stop."

"Are you on your way to the lodge? I can give you a ride."

For a long moment, she just looked at him. Did she want to ride with him? If anyone saw her in his car, she might get in trouble.

"I'll drop you right at the front or any—"

"Around the side of the building." Julie interrupted. "The employees have a separate entrance."

He nodded. "Of course. I'll drive you to the door."

She frowned slightly, biting her lip in concern.

"Or just around the corner, if you prefer. Or I can call a taxi for you," he added after another hesitation from her.

"A taxi won't be necessary," she said. She couldn't afford the expense or the extra minutes it would take to arrive. She pushed the door open wide, and hit the lock button before getting out. "I'll take your offer," she managed. "Thank you."

His expression relaxed. "You're welcome."

Julie followed him to his sedan and he held the passenger door until she was seated, then closed it softly and went around the front of the car.

The interior was comfortably warm and it smelled of new leather. Was this the new car smell people talked about? She'd never owned a brand new car in her life.

Once he sat behind the wheel, Julie became aware of another scent, subtle and masculine.

Attraction curled in her stomach, and she inched closer to the door, putting some distance between them. Why did he have to smell so good? As if being handsome wasn't enough.

Max started the car and pulled onto the road after checking over his shoulder.

"Why the reluctance?" He asked after a couple minutes of silence. "I'm going to the lodge anyway."

"It's better that I'm not seen with guests," she admitted. There wasn't a written rule about fraternizing with the guests, but since so many of them were celebrities or held high-end positions, the unspoken expectation was firmly in place.

"I won't get you in trouble. I can explain what happened."

That would be worse. "You can just drop me off on the north side."

"Is that the only reason you hesitated to take a ride from me?" He glanced at her. "Sorry. I'm being rude. You don't have to answer that."

Julie returned the glance. "I'd feel more comfortable if I could pay you for your trouble, or at least for the gas."

"You don't have to think of it like that. I was in a position to help, so I did."

"Still…" She let her shoulders slump. He didn't understand. He probably had employees doing things for him all the time. Julie had grown up with her mom struggling after the divorce, unable to do simple things because she wanted a man to take care of her. Mom still struggled, even after all these years.

Julie appreciated her independence too much, and letting a guy she barely knew do something for her made her feel indebted to him. Jared the Jerk had always wanted something in return. Max looked like a nice guy, but what if he came later to collect on the favor?

"I'll tell you what," he said, the corner of his mouth rising in a small smile. "Next time I need some help, you'll be the first one to know."

She eyed him suspiciously. "As long as it's nothing illegal, immoral, or expensive."

"Of course." He lifted his right hand off the wheel and extended it to her. "Deal?"

After a beat, Julie shook it. "Deal."

She quickly freed her hand, before the contact of his warm skin had a chance to wreak havoc on her feelings.

An amused smile lightened his lips for a moment, and Julie's cheeks flushed. Was she that transparent?

As promised, he drove past the front and parked away from the employee entrance.

Julie grabbed her purse.

"What about your car?" he asked.

"I'll call the insurance when I have my break. I want to wait and hear what they have to say first."

"That's wise."

She reached for the handle on the door, then turned to him. "Thank you for the ride. I do appreciate it."

"My pleasure, Julie."

His voice as he said her name. Julie almost closed her eyes. Was he aware of the effect it had on her? Did he do it on purpose?

As he drove away, she noticed the make and model of the car. How apt. She let out a humorless chuckle, suppressing an eye roll. How many times had she sighed at the scene in her favorite movie, when the dashing prince arrived on a white horse to save the woman he loved? Somehow, the memory rose in her mind and lingered in her heart for a moment too long.

Julie walked to the employee entrance, glad nobody was around to see how she had arrived. Slowly, her common sense came back. The car Max drove was white, and the similarities between her fantasy and the stark reality ended there. She was definitely not a heroine in need of rescuing; only a ride to work. Besides, Max was not a prince and he was not on a stallion, but driving a white Ford Mustang.

She could dream, but they would not be riding into the sunset together.

Life was never that good.

Chapter Four

Max entered the grocery store and found a cart. He swiped at the screen on his phone to verify his shopping list. From the corner of his eye, he saw Olsen enter the store. He usually gave Max more of a head start, but he also liked to vary his routine.

Henry was out at a bar in downtown Denver with a group of American friends, and Max had begged off with the excuse of a headache. It wasn't totally untrue. He would have developed a headache had he gone with his friend, who had much more stamina than Max did. Sometimes, their one-year age difference felt bigger than it really was, especially when Henry acted younger than his twenty-five years.

The truth was, Max was growing tired of the bar hopping routine. He didn't want to meet vapid girls and get buzzed. He wanted what he couldn't have—time with Julie to get to know her better.

He pushed the cart absently, the memory of Julie's guarded expression still fresh in his mind two days after he'd given her a ride to the lodge. Had she managed to get her car fixed? It was gone from the side of the road when he'd driven past earlier in the day. He'd worried about her, wondering how she'd gotten back home. After her hesitancy, he didn't want to push his company on her, not with her fearing a reprimand, or worse, the loss of her job.

Did the same rules apply outside of the Blue Mountain property? Julie had only said it was better not to be seen with him. But if she was off the clock and somewhere else, did he have a better chance to befriend her? Say, if they met while shopping at the grocery store? He could easily find out where she shopped, if he asked Olsen.

Max blew out a frustrated breath. He was doing it again. Premeditated friendship. He'd done it in school, planning how to be friends with other students in some way that didn't look too forced. Of course, in Markendom everyone knew who he was, and he hadn't felt like he'd made a true friend until Henry came along that one summer when he was nine.

At twenty-six years old, the line between casually bumping into someone and intentionally gathering information on her whereabouts was dangerously bordering on stalking, wasn't it?

Pushing the thought away, Max made his way to the bakery. This store was the only one in the area that carried rye bread with a texture and flavor closest to the authentic bread he missed from home. Making open-faced sandwiches without real ingredients didn't taste the same. He could probably have ordered one from the room-service at the Blue Mountain, but he enjoyed making his own.

He made a detour to the condiment aisle, considering the offers of ground mustard and mayonnaise. Maybe he'd have to find a Danish market after all.

"Hi, Mom, how are you?"

A feminine voice came from the aisle on the other side. At this time of night, with fewer shoppers in the store, and only the metal shelving and products in the way, the conversation came through clearly.

"I can't. My car broke down on Saturday—"

He didn't catch the last part of the sentence. His attention perked up, as he thought he recognized the familiar tone in the voice. It almost sounded like Julie. Was it really her? His pulse quickened at the possibility. What were the chances that she was shopping at the same store as him on a Tuesday night? Too much of a coincidence, but not impossible in a small town.

The conversation went on.

"—car is too old and too—" the woman paused.

"Yeah, I know, but it's no big deal. The bus is fine. When the weather warms up I can find an old bicycle and—" She said something else that was lost in the space that separated the two aisles.

Max picked up a random jar from the shelf and placed it in the cart to give his hands something to do. Heat crept up his neck. He'd reached a new low in his life, listening in on private conversations hoping it was Julie on the other side.

The impression stuck with him as he checked off the items on his list and placed them into the cart. Even as he tried to focus on what he was doing, thoughts of Julie followed him.

He lingered in the dairy section, by the imported butters and yogurts. The front of a cart pulled up next to him, and Max turned to excuse himself.

A slow smile pulled at his lips when he saw who it was. "Julie."

She wore a red sweater and dark skinny jeans, and her hair was down, curling in soft waves over her shoulders. Pony tails and chignons should be outlawed. Her hair was too glorious to be bound.

She frowned and her eyes went to the ball cap on his head, the one he'd worn to hide his blond hair.

Did she not recognize him? Max slid a hand to his head and pulled off the cap for a moment. "It's Max. We met at the Blue Mountain Lodge." He returned the cap.

"Yes, I know who you are…" Her words trailed off with hesitation.

"We're not at the Blue Mountain, Julie. You can call me by my first name." Max lightened his voice, hoping to set her at ease.

Her expression softened, an adorable smile pulling at her lips, despite the hint of reluctance in her eyes. "Hi, Max. How are you?"

Max grinned, the little thrill at hearing her say his name eclipsing everything else for a short second. "I'm well, thanks. And you? Did you get your car fixed?"

She bit her bottom lip and his eyes followed the gesture before meeting hers again.

She had full lips, kissable lips. One more detail about her to think over later.

"It was an old car." She shrugged.

He waited for more, but she didn't elaborate and he didn't ask. Maybe it had been her he'd heard talking earlier from the other aisle, which meant she still didn't have a car and was taking the bus.

"You shop here often?" he asked. Max cringed at his question, at his pathetic attempt to keep her for a few more minutes.

Julie gave him a bemused smile. "Often enough." She gestured towards the yogurts. "I can't resist the Galian yogurts. And you?"

"The butter. It's always the best. Trust me."

She nodded. "You should know. You're from

Europe, right? But not from Galia. You don't have the right accent."

Was she curious about him? How much could he tell her? If he told her he was from Markendom, she could get on Google and easily find pictures of the royal family. And she'd see him there, with his parents and older brother, sister-in-law, and young nephews.

Not that he was trying to keep it a secret, but he was enjoying that she treated him like a regular guy. No royal status to color her perception of him. He hadn't had that in a while.

"No, not from Galia," he replied. "But I've spent time there and I fell in love with the butter. And the fresh bread," he added.

Julie smiled again. "Galian bread and butter sounds divine. I'd go for it."

She glanced at the contents of his cart, her eyes dancing over each item before she looked back at him.

"Are you silently judging my shopping choices?" He asked, letting the amusement show in his voice.

A slow blush tinged her cheeks. "No judging, I promise. I remembered this line from a movie I saw once, where one of the characters said you can learn a lot about a person from looking in their shopping cart."

Max looked at his own cart with all the ingredients for open-faced sandwiches. "You might have a point there."

Julie's phone rang from inside her pocket. She grimaced, but didn't reach for it.

When the ring sounded again, he tipped his chin toward her. "Are you going to get that?"

She pulled it out and swiped at the screen. "It's my mom. I should take this. Sorry."

"Don't apologize," Max said. "Have a good night."

She waved at him over her shoulder and walked away as she answered the phone.

Max let out a long breath. He would have liked to keep talking with her.

Several minutes later, when Max arrived at the checkout lanes, she was there, a few spots ahead.

He watched her. She was distracted as she set the items on the belt, as if she had something heavy on her mind. A crazy thought flashed through him, wishing they were the kind of friends where he could ask her what was going on and she would tell him. He could almost see it. After sparing one last glance in her direction, Max shook it all away from his mind.

When he got to the front entrance, Julie stood to the side, her shopping bags at her feet. Heavy rain fell in relentless sheets, and the temperature had dropped enough to warrant a warmer jacket.

He took the bags and put the cart away, then stopped a few feet away from her. "Do you need a lift?"

Julie turned to him. "I'm just waiting it out." The corner of her mouth rose in a tired half-smile. "But thank you for the offer, Max," she added.

Was she waiting for the bus? How far was the bus stop? Max held the questions back and gave her a slight nod. If she thought he was going to drive away and leave her there—that was so not happening. But if he told her his plans, she'd probably leave before he got the chance to pick her up. He was sure she'd do it, from the little he knew about her.

He made a run for his car. There was an umbrella in the back seat, but he'd left it there, unaware the weather was fickle today. His hair was dripping and his jacket soaked by the time he entered the car. Max placed the shopping bags on the floor behind the passenger seat and removed the jacket, then turned the car on and cranked up the heat.

From his position, he could see Julie just inside the main doors. He sent a text to Olsen telling him of his plans so the man wouldn't wonder when Max left in a different direction. Max sat for a few minutes, and ran a hand through his hair, trying to get it somewhat dry.

When Max pulled up closer to the main entrance, he got the umbrella, opened it, then walked around the front of the vehicle until he stopped just outside the doors.

"Julie," he called her attention. "Come on, I'll give you a ride." He smiled at her, hoping his expression conveyed trust instead of weirdness.

For a long moment, she didn't say anything. Her eyes wandered from him, to the umbrella, to the car, and finally to the torrential pour that showed no signs of abating any time soon. In the end, it was the rain that made up her mind, Max was sure of it. From what he'd observed about her, she seemed to be a cautious, practical woman, and practicality won whatever internal battle she'd waged with herself just now. As guarded as she was, her gaze had shown enough of her thoughts during those seconds.

Her posture relaxed and she bent down to pick up the bags. Max opened the door and held the umbrella over her head while she entered, then he hurried to his side and slid behind the wheel.

He set off slowly, giving her the time to adjust. The interior was warm and her shoulders eased.

"Is this a new habit?" she asked, her attention on him.

Max frowned. "What?"

"You, coming to my rescue in your white charger." She looked away, as if the words had escaped without her consent.

He let out a low chuck. "You hardly seem like the type of woman who needs rescuing."

When her posture visibly tensed, Max realized his comment hadn't come out the way he'd intended. "That was a compliment. I'm sorry it didn't sound like one. I meant to say, you strike me as an independent and capable woman, not someone who's waiting for things to happen, or people to save you." He blew out a frustrated breath. "How about I shut up instead?"

A little smirk graced the corner of her mouth. "There's a small café around the corner that's open late and has the best hot chocolate. What do you say?"

"I say yes." He didn't have to be asked twice to spend more time with her.

Julie gave him directions. It wasn't far, like she'd said, but the opaque rain made visibility tricky, and he turned his focus to the road. He could feel her eyes on him, glancing covertly at first, then more confidently, brimming with curiosity and a sort of wonder. How many questions did she have, and how many did she hold back, keeping herself behind the walls she'd built around her?

Max wanted to have the chance to get close to Julie, but would she let him in?

Chapter Five

Julie brought the mug to her lips and sipped. The chocolate was rich and warm, and it filled all the worn-out spots in her. Or maybe it was the company. She smiled at Max, who held a mug of his.

Max was warm and comfortable like a cup of rich chocolate. Not that she would tell him that. Men didn't appreciate being called such, but she hadn't felt this way in a long time, if ever. When was the last time she'd sat with a guy who didn't pressure her for more?

Her track record with men was abysmal. In high school, she hadn't had the confidence to spend time with any guys, even for casual group outings. When she started college, it hadn't been much different at first, not until meeting Ashlyn at work. Her roommate had enough self-confidence for the both of them, and their friendship became a boon to Julie. By the time she met Jared, Julie had been ready for it, both socially and emotionally. He was charming at first, if not too demanding of her attention, and having no experience, Julie hadn't seen the warning signs. Who could have known he'd turn out to be so wrong on so many levels, so selfish and self-serving? When he didn't get from her what he wanted, he'd left, but not before inflicting the kind of wounds that weren't visible.

Sometimes, she doubted she'd recover the confidence and assurance of before, but sitting across from Max, she almost believed she could. Was it too much to wish he was a decent guy with more on his mind than money and sex?

He looked around the small space and motioned with his chin. "This is nice."

It was nice. Julie had loved the Cool Beans café since the first time she'd stepped inside. It was decorated with lots of wood accents and a wall of exposed brick, with round tables in the middle, and high-backed booths along the edge. They served coffee, chocolate, and tea every day, even in summer. "Which one, the chocolate or the space?"

His crooked smile made an appearance. "The chocolate is excellent, and the space is cozy, but definitely the company."

Hadn't she just been thinking the same thing?

His phone vibrated and Max winced. "Excuse me. I need to reply, or they'll call me instead." He swiped at the screen, tapped a short message, then slipped the phone into his coat pocket. "There. That should take care of it."

"Family responsibilities or business?" she asked.

"I'm in the family business, so it's a bit of both."

"Is that the reason for your trip?"

He shrugged. "In a way. I'm looking for investors in various fields. Henry has connections, so he's helping me."

"How long will you be staying in the U.S.?"

"It depends on how business goes. But enough about me." His eyes brightened.

Julie had been asking too many questions, enthralled by his voice and the way he put her at ease. "I'm sorry. I'm usually not so annoying." Her cheeks heated.

"Curious, not annoying. But since I want to learn more about you, now it's my turn to ask." He paused as if to gauge her reaction, and when Julie gave him a small nod, Max went on. "What are you studying?"

She raised an eyebrow. "How do you know I'm a student?"

Max blushed. "The other day, when your car broke down, I noticed your Denver University key chain." He raised his mug and took a long sip.

"Easy assumption, I guess," she said. "I'm studying to be a social worker."

"That is noble, hard work," he said, in a tone of respect.

"I'm not doing it for the money, that's for sure."

"Then why are you doing it?"

Julie had been asked this before, but something about Max's expression and the way he'd described social work as hard and noble gave her pause—hard, yes; noble, she wasn't so sure. That wasn't her. She didn't have any nobility in mind. She only hoped to make a difference, however small.

"My father left my mom and me when I was three years old," she started. "I don't have any memories of him, and she never told me much. I do remember bouncing from place to place, mostly friends' houses, and sometimes shelters or family centers. She also had a lot of boyfriends, and there was no stability of any kind whatsoever." She paused and took a drink from a glass of water she didn't remember asking for. Max looked at her still, unhurried and undemanding, his chin propped on his left hand and his attention on her. "When I was seven, she met this guy and we moved in with him shortly after, and a year later she gave birth to twin boys." Julie sighed. There was a lot more to the story, but so much of it was wrapped up in her relationship with her mother, Victor, and the boys.

"How old are your brothers?"

Julie met his eyes. Jayden and Jordan were her

half-brothers, but Max hadn't used the term, and somehow she knew it hadn't been an oversight. "They're fourteen." And always getting in trouble. "Victor, their dad, died in a car accident five years ago, and it hasn't been easy for them or my mother."

"Or you," Max said, his voice tender.

He was right, it hadn't been easy for her either. Going to school and working, making sure her grades were always high, earning her scholarship to Denver University, saving money for her needs and to send home—it hadn't been easy at all. Still wasn't.

Julie shrugged. "I remember all the social workers who tried to help us, the ones who had compassion, even when something got in the way of them being able to do anything more. They made a difference, and that's the goal I have. To help in any way I can, to be that difference in a child's life, even if only for a little bit."

"Julie," Max said. He reached for her hand and held it. His fingers were warm and his hand large, the weight of it a comfort to her. The gesture grounded her, made her feel connected and like she mattered. How was it possible? They hardly knew each other, and already there was a bond between them.

Or did she imagine it?

"I'm not telling you all this to get your pity, Max."

He shook his head. "You have my admiration. Not my pity."

She wanted to protest, but it would only bring more attention to her, and that was the last thing she wanted at the moment. The way Max noticed her, his hand still holding on to hers, already wreaked havoc with her mind and heart. Kindness, more than anything, spoke to Julie, and Max was kind. Combine that with his good looks and his deep voice, and Julie was well on her way to having a major crush on him. The butterflies in her stomach could attest to that.

Max's phone vibrated, and he let out a frustrated breath. He looked at the screen, but he didn't answer the phone. "I apologize for the interruption. They know better than to bother me after dinner time."

Julie straightened in her seat. "I've been monopolizing your time and attention, and you're too much of a gentleman to tell me to shut up." She reached for her jacket. "Besides, I have to get up early for a class I don't even like."

"I thought you get to choose the classes on your major," Max said. "Why did you pick classes you don't like?"

"Because I had a conflict in my schedule."

Max raised an eyebrow.

"In order to graduate, I need passing grades from all the classes, which includes the requirement for

Physical Education. Unfortunately for me, the only class that works with my schedule for this term is archery. It was either that or fencing, so I chose the one that seemed less dangerous."

"Less dangerous? How do you figure?"

"Well, in fencing the sword is coming at you. At least in archery the arrow is pointing away from you."

Max chuckled, a delicious low sound that triggered something in her. "You don't seem very excited about it."

"I'm failing an elective class. It's embarrassing." Julie sighed. "At this point, I'm desperate enough to consider hiring a tutor, if only I could find one with morals and within my budget."

"And you've been looking for tutors?"

"I made some inquiries. There was a guy who said he'd help me, but he wanted a sort of payment I'm not willing to give." A blush filled her cheeks and Julie looked away for a moment. Why did she always attract the creeps?

Max was everything the opposite so maybe her luck with guys was changing.

"How many times have you been to this class?" He asked.

"One practical lesson and two of theory. I had a little accident and I'm not looking forward to repeating." She pulled at her sleeve and exposed a welt that ran the length of her forearm.

Max winced. "Doesn't the coach provide arm guards? How important is this class?"

"Pretty important. If I fail, I won't be able to get the internship position I need for my training."

"I know someone who can help you bring your grade up in archery and he won't even ask for anything in return," Max said, pausing to look at her steadily.

Julie looked back at him. "No. I can't possibly—" She shook her head, not even surprised he was an archer, probably a great one too.

He reached a hand and touched her wrist. "Hear me out, Julie. I'm really good. Not trying to brag or anything. I can help you."

"I don't doubt you're good, but I can't let you do this."

"Not even if it'll get you the passing grade you need?"

Julie sighed. She wasn't in a position to say no, and he knew it. "Where will we practice? The course on campus is always booked."

A smile danced in his eyes. "I'll take care of it. Just bring your equipment."

Her expression fell. "The class provides the bows and arrows. I don't have any of my own."

"That won't be a problem. Don't worry." Max pulled out his phone. "What's your number?" After they exchanged numbers, Max looked up at her. "I'll give you a call when I have everything set up."

"I'll let you know when I have a time that works best." Julie pulled her wallet out.

"Absolutely not." Max covered her hand and stopped her. "This is on me."

"But I was the one to suggest we come here. That's what good manners say. The person who invites is the person who pays."

He watched her for a moment. "All right," Max conceded at last. "I'll accept that, but next time I'll do the inviting."

Did he want there to be a next time? Julie did. She wanted to spend more time with Max.

He drove her home. The rain had abated to a drizzle, the street lights casting long reflections on the wet pavement. She should be tired, but her time with Max had energized her instead. His company soothed her and excited her at the simultaneously.

He stopped in front of her apartment building. "Please wait." He exited and walked around the front of the car, opened the door for her and held the umbrella over her head. Julie got out with her bags and Max walked her to the building.

She held the bags in one hand and reached out her fingers to touch his arm with her free one. "Thanks, Max. For stopping and everything else. Even if I didn't need to be rescued," she teased.

Max watched her with an intense gaze, and his eyes flicked to her lips before returning up to look at her again. Julie stood rooted and held her breath, then extended her free hand to him. He took it, but instead of shaking it, he turned it in his and kissed her knuckles. At the contact of his warm lips on the back of her cold hand, Julie's skin turned into goose bumps, and a pleasant tremble shuddered inside her.

"My pleasure, Julie," he said.

And this time, she believed him.

Chapter Six

A knock sounded at the door of his cabin and Max walked over to open it.

Henry didn't wait to be invited in. "Maximilian, haven't seen you in a while."

It was a long running joke between them, Henry calling Max by his full name. Since Henry's name was short, Max couldn't reciprocate, and Henry had always thought it was too funny, especially since he was addressed as Prince Maxim in Markendom. His family and friends called him Max, and he preferred that too.

"I could say the same about you," Max replied.

He'd seen Henry in passing, but they hadn't met in a couple of days.

Henry's eyes fell on the equipment lying on the floor of the front room. "What are you up to?"

"Just helping out a friend." Max walked to the kitchen, eager to take the attention off the bows and arrows inside the partially open duffel bag.

"Does this friend have big brown eyes and shapely legs?" Henry smirked. "It's the waitress at the restaurant, isn't it?"

"What if it is?" Max's tone became defensive.

Henry raised his hands in a placating gesture. "Hey, I'm all for having fun, you know that. But there has to be something better than archery with a girl for a date."

"It's not a date. She's failing the archery class and I offered to help." Max opened the fridge and placed two cans of soda on the counter.

"Little does she know you're one of the top archers in your country." Henry popped the tab on his can and took a long swig. "You have something more planned, right?"

Max did have more planned, but that didn't mean he wanted to share it with Henry, even if he was his best friend. "I'm sure you didn't come over to give me dating tips."

"As much as you need them, I didn't." Henry reached in his back pocket and produced an envelope. "Official invitation."

Max took the cream envelope with the Durham seal. "To what?"

"The consulate's Spring event fundraiser. Alex got tangled in some nasty PR business involving an actress and the royal advisers have asked the embassies and consulates to organize opportunities for 'positive publicity.'" Henry added air quotes to the last two words. "It's just a way to take people's eyes and minds off what the tabloids are saying."

"Is Alex all right?" Henry's older brother was closer in age to Max's older brother, Sebastian. The Somerset middle brother, Stefan, was in Washington researching a cure for cancer, and Victoria, the younger sister, was at home in the royal palace with their parents.

Henry passed a careless hand through his hair. "He's with Nicholas in Galia, laying low until it all blows over."

Nicholas was the Galian crown prince, and a cousin to the princes of Durham. The Galian palace was probably the best place to get away from the public eye in Europe.

Max glanced at the invitation. "Penguin suits?" He and Henry had used the term instead of using the right words, black tie, when they were younger, and it had stuck as a private joke since then.

Henry smiled. "Definitely penguin suits. There will be lots of prominent names there, which means possible investors."

The schmoozing, as the Americans called it. Max wasn't fond of it, but it was necessary. "I'll be there. We'll be there, my plus one and I." He knew just who to ask, if he could convince her. Somehow, he suspected she'd resist.

"What's her name? I'll add her to the list."

"Julie Winters." She hadn't told Max her last name, but he'd asked Olsen, who always kept a file on anyone Max spent more than five minutes with, as a safety precaution. Max never asked to see any files, but this once he'd been too curious to know her full name.

Henry swiped at the screen and typed, then he nodded. "Good luck with your archery lesson."

"Thanks." Max would probably need it, even if he didn't admit it to Henry.

After Henry left, Max checked in with Olsen and related his plans for the evening and the next day. Clear communication with his private security detail was a good way to avoid problems on both parts. This way, Max could enjoy relative privacy and Olsen could do his job without getting too close.

He pulled out his phone and sent a text to Julie.

This is Max. Are we still on for tomorrow?

If she was busy, it would take her a few minutes to reply. It came just in five.

Hi, Max. Yes, we're on for tomorrow. It's my day off at work and I only have two classes in the morning. I'm free for the rest of the day.

Perfect. I'm looking forward to it. What time are you off today?

I should be done by five. I worked the early shift today.

Can I take you out to dinner tonight?

This time her reply took longer.

I wish I could. I have a study group session for sociology.

She typed a sad face and Max added one of his own in reply.

What about after the archery lesson? If I haven't accidentally shot you.

He smiled at her suggestion.

I'll be there with you. No accidents allowed. And yes, let's go out after, please.

Nothing fancy.

I can do casual.

You forget I've only seen you dressed in a suit.

Max remembered wearing a suit to the restaurant a couple of times, and apparently it had been enough to make an impression on Julie. Did that mean she liked seeing him wearing one?

Noted. No suit.

Now you're just putting words in my mouth. I didn't say that.

There was a lighter side of Julie in these texts and Max smiled. He liked it. Maybe she was beginning to feel more at ease with him.

So you do like the suit.

He couldn't resist teasing her.

If you're trying to get me to admit, it won't happen.

You're saying you like the suit, just not tomorrow.

He added a winky emoji.

Fine. No suit tomorrow. Where are we having the lesson?

At the country club. Can I come pick you up?

No, that's all right. I'll get there.

I'll wait for you at the side garden.

It was out of view from the main entrance and away from the comings and goings of the other guests and staff.

Will do. Good night.

Good night, Julie.

Max held the phone in his hand for another moment, waiting to see if Julie sent another text. After a few minutes, he stood and set the phone down on the coffee table, then rolled his shoulders and let out a long breath. He was developing a serious crush on her. When was the last time he'd been this interested in a woman?

Julie was different. Genuine. And she treated him like he was a normal guy. Around her, Max didn't feel the weight of his lineage and the responsibility of his status. To Julie, he was just Max, a guy from Europe visiting the United States. She didn't know of Prince Maxim, the fourth in line to the crown of Markendom, right after his older brother and his two nephews.

Sooner or later, he had to tell her, preferably before she found out from someone else, or saw something in the media. That wouldn't go well.

What would she say when she knew?

Chapter Seven

Julie sat on a park bench off the main path to the Blue Mountain Country Club. The garden had relative privacy and she felt comfortable there.

Ashlyn worked today and Julie had come with her, arriving earlier than the appointed time with Max. It would be a while before she could buy another car, and the city bus didn't come up to the lodge.

The day was clear and balmy enough to only wear a light jacket. Julie had brought her Kindle to read while she waited for Max, and she got lost in the book. The sounds of early spring around her, the sun warming her skin, the ebook in her hands—as good as it was, it would become much better when Max arrived. He was going to help her get a passable grade in archery, but more than that, they'd be spending time together.

Max pulled up in a golf cart, his hair delightfully blown from driving without a top, and his shirt sleeves rolled up to his elbows. What was it about a man's forearms that set something alight in her chest? At least, this man did.

He parked and jumped out, then raised his sunglasses past his forehead. "Julie." He said her name with a smile. "Are you ready for your private archery lesson?"

Julie tucked the e-reader in her purse and stood. "As ready as I can be." She was not as ready for spending time with him as she was for the lesson. Did that make her a hypocrite? He'd only offered to help because she'd complained about her failing grade. And here she was now wishing for more than to pass the Physical Education requirement.

Dressed in fitted jeans and a tailored dress shirt casually untucked, Max looked good. The blue of the shirt brought out the color of his eyes, the gray taking on a richer, deeper hue that mimicked the color of the sky today. All the little details about him had become prominent to her—the way his smile hitched a corner of his mouth, the crinkles around his eyes, the timbre of his voice when he said her name— and Julie found herself incapable of looking away, unwilling to slow down her thumping pulse, and unable to let her cheeks cool down. Her mind, her body, her heart took notice of Max and the excitement and fear took hold of her in equal measures.

Max reached for her hand and, for a moment, she thought he'd kiss the back of it as he had done before. The butterflies rose to the pit of her stomach. He squeezed her fingers and didn't let go until she took her seat beside his.

What if he could tell the way she reacted to him?

"We couldn't have asked for more perfect weather," he said after restarting the cart. "It's clear, it's sunny, and there's no breeze in the air."

"No breeze means less chance of arrows gone astray," Julie said. "I do know that."

"True. Not that we have to worry about errant arrows at the location I was able to secure."

Julie turned to look at him. "I don't think I've thanked you yet."

"I'm pretty sure you have."

"I'll say it again. Thanks for taking time off from your busy schedule to help me pass my class." He probably had more important things to do with his time. "I appreciate it."

"I'm glad to help. I hope you know that." He glanced at her. "And no strings attached."

"Well, if I don't succeed, it's the student's fault, not the teacher's."

"Let's have a little faith, okay?" He smiled again and something inside her melted. She loved his smile.

Max pulled out of the path behind the golf course and drove for another ten minutes until they came to a clearing facing the woods at the edge of the property. He parked and retrieved a long duffel bag from the back of the cart. A row of three targets was already set up.

Julie followed him. "How did you know about this place?"

Max knelt and unzipped the bag. "I explained to the concièrge what I needed and he set it up."

"He must have wanted to impress you." Julie looked around the location. The clearing was perfect, set far back from the golf course and with the kind of privacy where they could practice by themselves without anyone else around. She wouldn't have to worry about accidentally hitting someone.

She turned to Max and the equipment he'd brought. He removed two bows from the bag, a recurve and a compound, the first one long and graceful, and the second shorter and less elegant.

"You got me a compound bow." She'd studied about them in the archery theory textbook.

Max unpacked the arrows for each bow. "I want to see your draw length before bringing a recurve bow that will fit you."

Was Max planning a second lesson for her already?

"My draw length is pathetic," Julie said. "I can't draw the bowstring back far enough to properly loose the arrow."

"You seem to know the vocabulary pretty well."

They chatted about bows and arrows, and other archery terms, for a few minutes.

"Are you testing my knowledge?" Julie asked. "I passed the theory pre-test easily enough. It's the actual positioning and drawing that I can't get right."

Max smiled. "Is that your way of telling me to get started already?" He handed her an arm guard and a finger saver. "Get these on, please. They'll make it easier to avoid injuries."

When she was done, she picked up the bow and an arrow.

"Take your stance," Max said.

Julie positioned the bowstring and tried to draw it. This was one of the parts she had difficulty with.

Max moved behind her left side and set his hand on her elbow. "Too high. Elbow down a little bit."

Julie adjusted her arm as she tried to focus on properly shooting an arrow. Max stood close to her—too close. She could feel his body heat next to hers and every time he set a hand on her skin, goosebumps erupted unchecked. Was it her imagination or did something spark between them?

He continued, unfazed. "Next, you're going to use your mouth as an anchor for the correct height when loosing an arrow."

Julie lowered the bow. "Excuse me?" When she turned to Max, he'd come much closer than before.

His eyes flickered to her mouth and Julie looked at him and the contour of his lips. How did a guy have such perfect lips? Were they as soft as they seemed? If she turned her head a fraction more, she would know. She could kiss him and find out how soft his lips were—it would be so easy.

Max cleared his throat and took a small step back. Julie's cheeks flamed. Anxious to deflect the attention from her, she drew the bow with all her strength and let go. The arrow made a short arc and landed on the grass.

Maybe this archery lesson wasn't such a good idea.

"Okay, let's try it again." Max grabbed another arrow and handed it to her.

Julie took a deep breath and raised the bow, gaze firmly planted on the target. She would not look at his mouth this time. Or his eyes. Or the way his arm muscles corded when he moved.

Eyes on the target, not on Max.

Max stepped beside her, his right hand falling on her shoulder, his left covering her fingers that tightly clutched the grip.

"Relax, Julie." His voice was soft, and his breath fanned the side of her cheek.

She let go and the arrow landed by the target.

"That was so much better already," Max said with excitement in his voice.

"Marginally better," Julie replied. She might have closed her eyes for the breadth of a heartbeat.

Max helped her for another half hour and she worked on her stance and positioning, on drawing and releasing until she actually hit the target, even if it wasn't anywhere close to the center.

"When is your next class?" Max asked as he retrieved the arrows she'd shot.

"On Monday." Maybe she'd be able to show some improvement to her instructor.

"If you have time this weekend, I can meet with you so you can gain more confidence before then." He opened the duffel bag and set the compound bow inside.

"No, I can't ask you to spend more time with me on this," she protested. For sure he had better things to do.

"You're not asking. I'm offering. There's a difference, you know." The merriment in his eyes caused her heart to skip another beat. "Send me a text tomorrow and we'll set up another time to meet."

"I feel like I'm taking advantage of your generosity, Max," Julie said.

"You're not. Where I'm from, friends help friends without an expectation of return."

"Is that what we are, friends?" She asked the question before censoring herself.

He looked at her, a long, searing glance that added an extra beat to her heart. "Friends for now. Maybe good friends in the future?"

He posed it as a question, but it didn't sound as one to her ears. His expression was too assured.

"Are you going to show me your archery skills?" Julie asked, hoping to distract the attention from her.

"As long as you don't think I'm showing off."

"Of course not." Any other guy would be more than happy to flaunt it, but in the short time she'd known Max, she'd come to learn he was not the kind of guy to bring unwanted attention to himself.

Max retrieved the recurve bow and an arrow. His stance was perfect and when he drew then let go, the arrow flew straight and hit the target dead center.

"That was perfect," she said in awe.

"Nearly perfect. I'm a bit distracted today." He winked at her.

Did he mean to imply she was the distraction?

Chapter Eight

Max couldn't remember the last time he'd had such a fun afternoon. Julie was the kind of genuine, undemanding woman he didn't even know he'd been looking for. She'd been surprised to hear he considered them to be friends, but he wanted much more than friendship with her. He was falling for her, fully and fast, and he didn't want to hold back from it.

After stowing the duffel bag with the archery equipment in the back of the golf cart, Max reached into the middle seat and got out the picnic hamper and blanket.

Julie stood to the side, watching him. "Is that what I think it is?" Curiosity laced her voice.

Max carried the large basket and handed the blanket to Julie as she walked beside him.

"You know how I asked to take you out to dinner

after the archery lesson?" Max glanced at her. She nodded. "Well, I really meant outdoors."

A large smiled bloomed on her face. "Like a real picnic?"

"I can tell you it's not a fake picnic." Max grinned, charmed by her genuine enthusiasm.

He found a spot at the edge of the clearing by a mature oak tree and set the hamper down on the wild grass. Julie unfurled the blanket and he helped spread it straight, then they both sat on it.

Julie sat with her legs crossed and overlooked the clearing toward the golf course and the lodge. "When I was seven, my mom had a job for about six months and we lived in an apartment around the corner from a neighborhood park. On the weekends, I'd walk over, sit on the swings, and watch the families eating together at the picnic tables." A look of melancholy came over her face and she closed her eyes briefly, as if to put the memory away.

Max didn't know what to say. He didn't have to ask to know she'd never had a picnic with her mom—the answer was in her eyes and posture. An overwhelming sense of affection came over him. He wanted to take her in his arms and hug her—hug grown-up Julie and young Julie and tell them both they'd be okay; hug them until they knew he was there for them. She'd had a rough childhood, and from some of the comments she'd made, it seemed that her life was still not easy. Maybe there was something he could do to make it a little better for her.

"I'm sorry, Julie," Max said, as a way of acknowledging he'd heard her.

"What did you bring?" she asked with a smile that somehow didn't reach her eyes.

She seemed ready to let go of the subject, and Max followed her cue. "A tour of European flavors," he replied.

He opened the hamper and started removing the items, describing them as he set them down. "Fresh bread and butter from Galia, *jamón* from Aragonia, a selection of cured meats and cheeses from Germany and Holland, smoked salmon from Markendom to make open-face sandwiches, and Portuguese egg custard tarts for dessert." He grabbed a bottle and two glasses. "And to drink, Italian soda." He'd also brought fresh fruit and her favorite Galian yogurts.

She leaned forward, still smiling. "My goodness, you went all out. And you remembered our talk about food at the grocery store. How did you get all this?"

"I have some contacts who have some contacts," he said, pulling out the plates and silverware. "But it's all legal," he rushed to add.

Julie chuckled. "I'm sure it is. It's not like there's a black market for European food, is there?"

"You'd be surprised," Max said. He sure missed the European cuisine.

Julie filled her plate with a little of everything. "I don't know where to start. It all looks so good." She took a bite of the egg tart and closed her eyes.

Max watched her. "You eat dessert first?"

"What if I get too full with everything else? Then I won't have room."

"You're right." Max picked up a tart and bit into it. "I haven't had one of these in a while. So delicious."

They chatted about their likes and dislikes, and Max felt a stirring in his heart. The more he knew about Julie, the more he wanted to know. He observed her while she talked, taking the time to notice how she reacted to their topics of conversation, how she replied to him, the way she didn't agree with everything he said while explaining what she believed in. She had her own opinion and was able to defend it respectfully. She told him about her classes, the things she was learning, and the plans she had for the future, and Max told her of his travels and the people he met. In the back of his mind, he knew he needed to tell her who he was, but decided to wait until he took her home.

Even after they'd eaten and packed the hamper, they lingered on the blanket, unwilling to leave. The afternoon stretched before them, colored with the beginnings of the setting sun, and still they sat side by side, slipping into a comfortable silence.

A chilly breeze rose from the woods behind them, and Julie rubbed her arms.

"Are you ready to go?"

She turned to him. "Not yet."

He wasn't either. Max moved nearer. "Come here." He wrapped his arms around her and brought her closer to him. She came willingly, naturally, with her back to his chest. "Better?"

Julie relaxed against him and her hands rested on his forearms. "Much better. Thank you."

Something changed as a conscious feeling rose between them. He was aware of all the points where their bodies touched, aware of her warmth and scent, of the way she fit tucked against him. His breathing synced to hers, and he wanted to stay like this forever.

"Julie." He whispered in her ear.

She stirred and he adjusted his embrace so she could better turn in his arms to face him.

He didn't plan it when his lips touched hers. He drew back, but Julie met him again without a trace of hesitation. The kiss started slow at first, exploratory, until it crescendoed into something more, something deep and warm, and with a promise of even more to come.

They both wanted it, both sensed the rightness of it. He knew it and he knew Julie knew it as well.

They fit together and this kiss was only the beginning of it. The realization thrilled him.

After a few seconds or a few minutes, he couldn't tell, they eased away from the kiss fractionally, their arms still holding on to each other. The words didn't come right away, but words hardly mattered when so much more had passed between them.

When a hint of darkness tinged the sky, Max rose and extended his hand to Julie. He took the hamper to the golf cart and she folded the blanket. When they met beside the cart, he opened his arms and she settled there. Max kissed her forehead and she sighed.

"When can I see you again?" he asked.

"Tomorrow I have school and then the late shift at the restaurant."

"I won't come to the restaurant," he said.

Julie visibly relaxed. He understood why she didn't want him there. "I'll wait for the end of your shift," he said.

She nodded.

"And the rest of the week?" Was he too greedy to want to see her every day?

Julie pulled out her phone and he did the same, comparing their schedules.

"It's my day off next Friday, but I'm going to see my mom and the boys in the morning," she said.

He remembered the invitation Henry had given him. "There's an event that night I have to attend and I'd like you to come with me." Very much.

Julie bit her bottom lip. "What kind of event?"

"A party some friends of Henry are hosting,

something he arranged for him and I to come." Max downplayed it. "For the business contacts." He could sense her hesitation.

"How fancy is it?" she asked.

"Some fancy food and some fancy dancing, but we can slip off early and go somewhere else. What do you say? Can I pick you up?"

"How about I meet you there?"

Max nodded. "I'll text you the address and I'll make sure your name is on the guest list."

"Okay, I'll come," she agreed at last.

"Thank you, Julie." He hugged her close and kissed her lightly on the lips. He couldn't get enough of her, of saying her name, of holding and kissing her. If he deepened the kiss, he'd have a hard time letting her go. "Let's return the cart and I'll drive you home."

Max took the longest way back to the lodge, reluctant to see their wonderful afternoon come to an end.

Julie looked at him and shook her head, good-naturedly. "You're incorrigible," she said with a smile.

Max chuckled and reached to squeeze her hand.

When they arrived, he parked, then handed Julie out. A lodge attendant came to take the cart and Max took Julie's hand as they walked the short distance to the valet parking to retrieve his car. As they rounded the building, a crowd fell on them, yelling and pushing. What was happening?

"Prince Maxim, is this your new girlfriend?" He heard the question shouted from different directions. The media had found him.

Julie tensed beside him and Max tightened his grip on her.

Olsen appeared out of nowhere. "This way, Your Highness."

Max took Julie by the elbow and tucked her to his side, shielding her from the onslaught of cameras and microphones, the shouts and the flashes firing unceasingly.

Julie turned to him slowly, not even resisting the gentle pressure as he propelled her forward, a deep frown in her expression and a look of unbelief in her eyes.

He was losing her already.

They entered the building through a service door. "Olsen, we need a private room ASAP."

"Yes, Prince Maxim," Olsen replied.

Within seconds, Olsen had cleared a small, empty office, once again proving the super-efficiency he'd built his reputation on.

Max entered, still holding on to Julie, half-fearing she would bolt, if given the chance.

"Prince Maxim," she said, pulling away from him when Olsen closed the door behind them. She closed her eyes for a moment, then opened them, an intense look in her expression. "You're a prince? H-How?

When were you going to tell me?"

Max rubbed the back of his neck. "I'm sorry you had to find out this way, Julie. I had plans to tell you. Today, in fact." He'd planned to tell her in the car when he took her home, so they could have more privacy.

He pulled out a chair for her, but she remained standing, arms crossed. Every time he took a step toward her, she stepped back. Max forced himself to stand in one place, hoping it wouldn't create any more distance between them.

"Where are you from exactly?"

"I'm from Markendom."

"Markendom," she repeated, shaking her head. "You're the crown prince of Markendom."

"Actually, my older brother Sebastian is the crown prince."

She frowned. "So you're the next in line."

He shook his head. "I'm the fourth in line. Sebastian has two young boys, three and five years old."

"You're the fourth in line to the throne of Markendom," she stated. "Why didn't you tell me? I can't understand that." She paced and turned away from him, a nervous energy in her steps, putting more and more distance between them as if she could not stand his presence.

Max winced at the accusation in her eyes. "Please, Julie, let me explain."

She squared her shoulders and turned to the door. "I need to leave. Will you please let me leave?"

"Yes, of course you can leave. I'll have Olsen drive us back."

"No," she said with finality, shaking her head again. "I want to leave alone."

He nodded slowly. "Let me find someone to escort you back."

Max sent a text to Olsen and within minutes someone from the lodge staff knocked at the door to take Julie.

"Can I call you later?" he asked before she left.

Julie paused, her back to him. "I don't think so. And find another date to the event."

She looked over her shoulder at the last moment, and the hurt and betrayal he found in her eyes were almost too much to take.

What had he done? How could such a perfect day end so badly?

Chapter Nine

Julie sat at the corner of the sofa, her legs tucked to the side and a fluffy blanket on her lap. The tea had since gone cold, but she still held the mug in her hands.

After a few days of sunshine and higher temperatures, the rain had returned, bringing with it the cold of a lingering winter. Never mind the calendar said it was spring.

It reflected her mood, this weather.

It had been five days since Julie had seen Max. They'd had the best time together that day. He'd been patient with her through the archery tutoring, going over the stance and positioning as many times as she'd needed, and by the end she'd shown a bit of improvement already.

Then he'd surprised her with the picnic and the wonderful food. So much thought had gone into everything he'd planned that day.

And the kiss.

Julie closed her eyes, reliving those moments. She could still feel his lips on hers, the solidity of his chest beneath her palms, his masculine scent she'd rather forget.

If she'd had any doubts before, she knew in that moment she was falling in love with Max.

But it had all come crashing down too quickly when they'd been accosted by the paparazzi.

Max was a prince, a bone-fide member of the royal family of Markendom.

Ashlyn had googled after Julie had told her everything, and she'd shown Julie the pictures of the royal family—Max with his parents, with his older brother and his wife, and their two adorable blond boys. A beautiful family and a popular leader, from what Ashlyn had read to her. The people loved King Frederik, Max's father.

Julie had also found Max's full name. Maximilian Frederik Torvald Christian Wolfe. Prince Maxim, as he was lovingly referred to by the people of Markendom. Second son and fourth in line to the throne.

He was a prince and he hadn't told her. How could she ever fit in his life, a commoner from America? He belonged to European royalty, in a country she hardly knew anything about. Her life was the opposite of his.

That was reality. What she thought she could have had with Max was only a dream.

He'd called her and texted her, had come by to see her, but she hadn't been ready to see him then, and had asked Ashlyn to run interference. After that, he'd sent flowers with notes asking to let him explain, but Julie hadn't responded. She hadn't responded to anything from him. But after almost a week without seeing him, she'd begun to question her reasons for not wanting to let him explain.

At the sound of the front door unlocking, Julie wiped an errant tear. If only she could stop crying.

Ashlyn walked in, took a good, long look around and groaned. "It's enough, Julie." She walked to the window and pulled up the blinds. "I've given you enough time to sulk and pine and feel sorry for yourself." Ashlyn came closer and took the mug from Julie's hands, then dragged the blanket off her legs, and sat beside her.

Julie remained seated in her corner.

"It's time," Ashlyn said.

"For what?" Julie's voice croaked, probably from all the crying she'd done recently.

"You're going to take a shower and make yourself presentable, and then we're going shopping."

Julie shook her head. "I don't have to go back to work until tomorrow." She'd asked her supervisor for a day off, and the lodge had only been too eager to see her away until the media frenzy died down and gave her three days instead. They hadn't commented on the fact she'd been with Prince Maxim, and she had to wonder if he'd had anything to do with that. With her day off in between, Julie hadn't needed to return since last week. Tomorrow was soon enough. "I don't want to go anywhere else."

"Wrong answer," Ashlyn said. "Isn't that party the day after tomorrow? The one Max invited you to?"

"I'm not going, Ashlyn. I told him that."

Ashlyn took her hand. "Julie, look at me."

Julie raised her eyes to meet her friend's.

"I know you might not agree right now, but you need to give Max a chance to explain himself. After everything that happened between you two, you won't find closure until you talk."

"Closure is overrated." Julie tugged her hand back, but Ashlyn didn't let go.

"Your pain is blinding you right now," Ashlyn said in a soft voice. "What he did was wrong, and he should have told you, but he might have his reasons and I think you need to hear him."

Julie shook her head again, but didn't comment, her resolve beginning to wane. Maybe Ashlyn was right.

"Regret is a hard price to pay for pride, Julie. Don't trade your heart for stubbornness."

Julie wiped the corner of her eyes, turning Ashlyn's words in her mind. Was she being stubborn?

The past few days had been hard without seeing him. After the initial shock of discovering he was a prince, Julie had been hurt that he hadn't trusted in her. Staying away from him had been easier in a way. But what if he had a good reason for not telling her? As much as their friendship was new and they'd just started to know each other better, Julie had believed the connection between them was growing, but now she doubted everything. Maybe it was time to give him a chance to explain himself, if he still wanted to.

"What if he won't talk to me?" Julie asked.

"From what you've told me about him, I don't believe he would do that. But if he does—and you can't blame him after your silence over the past few days—then you say your part while he listens, and at least you'll know you tried."

Ashlyn turned her palm. "Where's your phone? Let me read again what he said about the party."

Julie grabbed her phone from the side table and swiped at the screen, then handed it over to Ashlyn.

"He says black tie, Julie." Her voice rose with enthusiasm.

"Well, that does it. I don't have anything to wear."

Ashlyn pierced her with a look. "It's too bad you don't have a friend and roommate who's a fashion major." She pulled out her own phone and punched a number. "Anthony, it's Ashlyn. How are you, dear?

Listen, my friend is in need of something special for a black tie event. Do you still have that item I was raving about last week? You do? Please be a dear and hold it for me." She paused. "I know, I'll owe you big time. We'll be there in an hour."

She hung up and pulled Julie from the sofa. "Come on. A five minute shower."

"Who's Anthony?" Julie asked on her way to the bathroom, unable to keep her curiosity in check.

"He's the manager at Re-Threadz, the second-hand store with the best donations in Denver. I saw something there last week that I'm positive will look fabulous on you."

Nobody did fashion like Ashlyn, who had a talent to repurpose second-hand designer label clothing that others no longer wanted.

Two hours later, Ashlyn had haggled down the price of a 70s wedding dress with a hideous chapel train, a black dress from the 50s with a stained bodice, and a red silk scarf with a cigarette burn at one end.

Anthony, who wore his dark hair slicked back with shiny pomade and had bright purple polish on his nails, took a look at Ashlyn's choices and shook his head. "I should charge you more for these castoffs." He turned a look at Julie. "Is it for her?"

Ashlyn's hair bounced with barely contained enthusiasm. "She's going to a ball with a prince."

Julie slapped Ashlyn's arm, warning her to keep quiet.

"She will look better than Cinderella," Anthony said, with an expression that told Julie he didn't believe her friend, which was probably a good thing.

When Julie saw the total, her eyes widened in shock. Even with reduced prices for worn pieces, it was out of her budget. "I can't afford this, Ashlyn," she whispered.

Ashlyn waved a hand. "This is my formal wear project for the semester. I just need someone to model it for me and you'll do nicely." She winked. "I'll get an A plus, guaranteed."

Be that as it may, Julie planned right there to work some extra shifts to pay Ashlyn back.

When they returned to the apartment, Ashlyn brought out her sewing machine, dragged the furniture from the middle of the room, and set a working station on the coffee table. She took Julie's measurements, then began cutting and pinning and sewing, surrounded by yards and yards of black and white fabric.

Julie went back to work the next day. Apart from a few of her co-workers glancing at her covertly, everything was back to normal. At school, two girls she didn't know tried to talk to her about Max, but Julie ignored them.

On Friday, she attended one class, took the first shift at the restaurant, and arrived home right after lunchtime. Ashlyn was asleep on the sofa. On a padded hanger, suspended from the door jamb, was the most stunning dress Julie had ever seen.

The bodice was white lace, with long sleeves and a high neckline, and a red sash at the waist contrasted with the floor-length ball-gown black skirt. Julie approached and touched the top and the bottom with reverent fingers. "Wow," she said.

"You need to try it on for any last minute adjustments, but I don't think I'll need to make any. It's my best work ever."

"You're awake." Julie turned to her friend. She'd seen Ashlyn work almost non-stop for the last few days.

"I was just resting my eyes."

Julie looked to the dress again, unable to keep her gaze away from it. "What's underneath the skirt to make it billow like that?"

"Yards and yards of cheap black tulle. It's super scratchy so I made a black satin slip to wear close to the skin. Come on, go change out of those clothes. You'll find the half-white half-black slip on your bed."

"Ashlyn, I have no words." She would never be able to repay her.

Ashlyn stood. "Good. Max will be speechless too when he sees you wearing it."

Julie wasn't so sure. Most likely Max was used to seeing pretty girls, the kind with noble titles and diamond jewelry around their necks, wearing dresses that cost thousands of dollars.

As beautiful as the dress Ashlyn had made was, the little voice of worry niggled at the back of Julie's mind, the one that said she was only playing dress-up and deluding herself. Even though Max was the prince, she definitely was not Cinderella. But she had to find out for sure. She had to go and talk to him, listen to him—for closure, like Ashlyn had said. Julie definitely didn't want to grow old regretting her stubbornness.

"Argh, I can see you over-thinking this." She gave Julie a gentle push toward the bathroom. "Change of plans. Go shower, then we'll start with hair and make-up. The sooner you get out the door, the better."

Julie swallowed past her insecurities.

What if it was too late and Max wouldn't see her?

Chapter Ten

Max checked his cuffs and stretched his neck.

A server came by with several flutes of champagne on a platter, and Max grabbed for one. He didn't want to be here, but necessity held him to his responsibilities. Henry had gone to great lengths to secure the presence of several individuals who could prove beneficial for the investments Max sought. But his head wasn't in it.

One more hour. Max would give it another hour of his best effort. He'd walk and talk, and make sure he saw all the important people, maybe dance with a couple of their wives, and then he'd leave through a back door. That was all he had stomach for tonight.

He let out a long breath, laden with frustration and regret. Julie should have been at his side. He'd planned to talk, and flirt, and dance all night long with her. Everything else would have been a breeze to put up with if she'd been on his arm.

But she wouldn't see him, and hadn't even let him explain the reason why he hadn't told her about his identity and family duties. After trying to contact her for many days, he'd reluctantly given up.

Henry approached him. "How are you holding up?"

"Good, good."

"Liar." Henry called him on it. "You look miserable."

"Thanks, I like you too," Max replied, using their usual banter they'd started as youths.

"Have you heard from her?" Henry asked.

Max shook his head.

"And you won't try again?"

Max's shoulders sagged. "There comes a point when contacting her so much becomes harassment, doesn't it?"

Henry shrugged. "I guess it depends on how much she likes you and how much you like her."

Max liked Julie a lot, but he also had to protect his heart before he fell more deeply for her, especially without the chance of seeing his affections returned when she wouldn't even see him.

"When are we supposed to leave to Chicago?" Max asked, eager to change the subject.

"I've been meaning to talk to you about that," Henry replied. "I'm thinking we might just go straight to New York when you wrap everything up here."

"Sounds fine by me," Max said, relieved to hear the suggestion. "I don't have anything else holding me here in Denver." Not anymore.

Henry pinned him with a long look. "Well, just think about it. We don't have to leave tomorrow. There's a few prospects that might be worth exploring."

Did he mean business or Julie?

Max didn't have the heart to find out.

They stood there for a moment, each of them turned to his own thoughts as they watched the dancing couples.

"Are you ready for some introductions?" Henry asked at last.

Max straightened. "Let's do it."

Chapter Eleven

When Julie and Ashlyn arrived at the location, Julie gaped. It was a mansion, surrounded by high walls and an ornate gate. The sign outside read The Royal Consulate of Durham.

"Is this the right address?" Ashlyn asked.

Julie pulled out her phone and read the details Max had sent the week before. "That's what Max sent me." The invitation had said the dress code was black tie, but Max had failed to mention the name of the place. It shouldn't surprise her, now that she knew he was a prince.

"How exciting!" Ashlyn said.

At the sight of the guards at the gate and the long line of limos circling around the drive, Julie swallowed, all the previous doubts rising in force.

"I can't do this." She took a deep breath, willing her pulse to calm down, but failing miserably.

"Yes, you can." Ashlyn said. "We already talked about all the reasons why you need to do this, so get out there and do it." She exited the car and came around to open the passenger door to Julie.

Julie stood on tremulous legs and Ashlyn swatted at the skirt. "To shake the wrinkles out." Her expression softened. "You have to talk to him, or you'll always regret you didn't."

"Yes, I know." Julie nodded. She did have to do it, even if she felt like it was too much. She squared her shoulders and tucked the clutch under her arm, then lifted her full skirt so she wouldn't trip.

"Send me a text when you're ready to return home," Ashlyn said. "But I'm thinking you'll get a ride from Prince Max." She winked and climbed back inside the car.

Julie crossed the street when the light turned green. When she looked back at Ashlyn, she'd already left, probably to make sure Julie didn't change her mind.

One of the guards at the gate to the Durham consulate stepped forward from the side. "May I see your invitation, miss?" He had the typical Durham accent.

"I—I don't have one," she said. "I'm supposed to be on the list."

"What is your name, miss?"

"Julie Winters."

What if Max had removed her name from the list? He'd said her name would be there, but that was before she'd told him she wasn't coming.

The guard pulled out a tablet and tapped a finger several times. "Your ID, please, Miss Winters."

Julie opened her small clutch and handed over her driver's license.

The man passed the card through a portable scanner then signaled another guard. "Have a good evening, Miss Winters." He returned her ID and Julie put it back.

"This way, miss," said the second man. This one wore a black suit instead of a uniform, like he was secret service and not military. He led her to a tent where a woman in a black pantsuit took Julie behind a private partition, then waved a scanning wand at her, like the kind that TSA used at the airports. When done, the woman knelt on the floor and scanned under Julie's skirt.

Julie blushed, not knowing what to say. The woman rose, patted down the layers of tulle and straightened the fabric of the skirt on all sides, apparently satisfied with what she had found, or not found, under Julie's dress.

"Thank you, Miss Winters."

Julie only nodded, not knowing what to say in reply after the indignation of a search of her under clothes. A necessary precaution, but very unpleasant. If Ashlyn were here, she would have laughed and brushed off the whole thing.

Another man in black appeared at her side. "Welcome to the Durham consulate, Miss Winters."

She followed him to an elevator, and he pushed a button. They rode in silence and when the doors opened, two floors up, he motioned for her to exit. "Enjoy your evening, miss."

Julie mumbled her thanks and walked down a short hallway where another man wearing black tails and white gloves opened a set of double doors to her. She half-expected him to scream her name, like the royal crier did in the Cinderella movie but he only nodded at her as Julie went through.

Already this was the strangest night of her life. She only hoped she could find Max without having to ask someone where he was. She'd give it her best try and then leave.

Julie found herself at the top of a wide marble staircase. Somewhere, the sounds of an orchestra played the rhythmic strains of a waltz and the large, circular room below teemed with people dressed in black tie, the women in lavish dresses and the men in elegant tuxedos. A chandelier shone brightly from the ceiling, casting colored refractions at the domed walls.

What was she doing here? A moment of panic flared through her. She was so out of her element.

This was the world Max belonged to, and if she wanted a chance with him, she'd have to get used to the formality and ceremony. She passed her hands at the side of her ball-gown skirt and inhaled a deep breath, letting it out slowly. Please, please, please—let her find Max before she did something to embarrass herself.

She closed her eyes for a short moment, and settled a hand over her middle. She'd come this far, she might as well keep going until it ended.

At first, she couldn't find Max in the sea of men all dressed the same, black and white everywhere, interspersed with flashes of color worn by the women, but at the second sweep of the room, she became aware of two tall men talking to each other, one with dark hair and the other blond. The dark-haired one looked up with a crooked smile on his mouth, then tapped his friend on the arm.

Max turned, meeting her eyes.

He wore a black tuxedo, tailored to fit him perfectly. She'd never seen him looking so handsome, and the attraction she remembered flamed back to life. If this was the way she reacted at the sight of him, she was in so much trouble.

Julie descended the marble steps, glad the original owner of the skirt had been nearly her own height and Julie could wear a sensible pair of shoes instead of the stilettos Ashlyn had pushed her way. Tripping and falling down the stairs at the Durham consulate was the kind of attention she didn't want.

Max came forward until he stopped in front of her. He bowed. "Miss Winters." His expression was unreadable.

Was he mad she'd come and did he want her to leave?

Julie curtsied. Bless Ashlyn for insisting Julie practiced a proper curtsy. "Prince Maxim," she said, meeting his eyes as she rose from her position.

Max's friend appeared in her line of sight.

"Where are your manners, Max? Introduce me to this lovely creature."

"You remember Henry?" Max gestured to his friend.

She curtsied again. "Your Highness," she said.

Max's friend took her hand and brushed a barely-there kiss on the back. "Miss Winters, it's a pleasure to see you here. I hope this means Max can stop moping around the corners with a long face."

"Hey now," Max said, elbowing his friend. "I don't mope."

"He does," Henry whispered in a conspiratorial tone.

"I moped too," Julie replied in the same tone, with a small nod of acknowledgment.

"Change of plans," Max said, grinning at Prince Henry.

His friend chuckled. "I figured as much when I saw her at the top of the staircase. We'll talk later." He excused himself.

Max nodded, then turned to her. "May I have the pleasure of this dance, Miss Winters?"

A delicious shiver ran through her. Julie took his proffered arm and Max guided her to the center of the room, where some of the other couples gave them a wide berth.

"Everyone's looking at you," she whispered.

"Believe me, they're looking at you, not me." His eyes shone with an emotion she hadn't seen before. "You look exquisite, Julie."

Her cheeks flamed and her breath hitched.

He led her in wide circles, matching his steps to her much simpler ones. It wouldn't surprise her to find out he was a skilled dancer. Most surely, European princes had a well-rounded education that included ballroom dancing and archery.

"I missed you," he said. "I'm so glad you came."

She breathed a sigh of relief. He wasn't mad at her after all. "I missed you, too," she whispered.

There was more she had to say. "I came to apologize, Max. I'm sorry I didn't want to listen to you before. I'd like us to talk, if that's okay with you."

"I'd like that too," Max said in reply. "After this dance. I'm enjoying having you in my arms too much."

Julie's lips parted in a contented sigh. She was enjoying it just as much, if not more. It felt right to be in his arms. Barely a week had gone by and she'd missed him so much.

Max groaned. "If you keep looking at me like that, I'll kiss you right here in front of everyone."

"I don't know what you're talking about," she replied. But she did because she felt the same way about him.

Max looked at her as if she were the most precious thing to him, and she very much wanted to kiss him with the same passion she saw in his blue-gray eyes.

She breathed in, hoping to distract herself for a few more minutes. "You failed to mention your best friend is Henry Somerset, third in line to the kingdom of Durham."

Max squirmed. "We don't go about calling ourselves prince of this or prince of that, and sometimes we honestly forget. I never meant to be dishonest with you, Julie. You have to believe me." He let out a long breath. "I get so tired of women wanting to be with me because I'm Prince Maxim of

Markendom. When I met you, I could just be Max the man, not Maximilian the prince. It was freeing." He paused. "There are too many eyes on us and too many ears around. Come with me."

He held her hand tightly, and they weaved between the couples on the dance floor until they reached a set of French doors leading to the patio. Once outside, Max laced his fingers with hers and she stuck to his side down a short flight of stairs that opened up to an avenue of short trees.

"A formal garden," she said, unable to hold back the surprise and admiration in her voice.

Max chuckled low. "It kind of goes without saying. It's the Durham consulate. Durhams cannot live without their patterned hedgerows and architectural rosebushes."

At the end of a brick path, a neo-classic stone gazebo stood in the center of the formally designed garden. Light posts cast sufficient light around them, and they strolled hand in hand toward the central structure.

"When do you have to go back to your country?" she asked, hoping her voice didn't give away her fears.

Max stopped and turned her to face him, settling a hand on her waist. "You have another year before you graduate, right?"

Julie nodded, too distracted for words with the nearness between them.

"Then I'll stay for another year," Max said.

"You will?" she whispered.

"There's a company here in Denver that has the kind of investment we're looking for. I have to talk to my father first, but I believe it's perfect for my family's interests. I can work here and develop the contacts to get the project started and implemented in my country." He brought her closer. "I want to get to know you better, Julie. Spend more time with you. Do you think that's possible?"

"I'd like that too, Max." Julie slid her hands past his lapels and set them on his chest, the crisp fabric of his white dress shirt too thin to disguise the rapid beating of his heart. Hers beat with the same staccato rhythm, almost in tune with Max's.

He nuzzled the side of her cheek and kissed her neck just below her ear. Julie closed her eyes and trembled.

"You know, my father's royal advisers will insist on a public announcement," Max said, his breath sending her skin into goose bumps.

As Max lay a row of tiny kisses at the line of her jaw, Julie found only one word in reply. "Announcement?"

"Prince Maxim of Markendom is officially dating Miss Julie Winters, his royal girlfriend," he said with a smile.

"You mean that?" she asked in a soft murmur.

Max kissed the corner of her mouth. "Julie, will you be my girlfriend?"

"If I say yes, will you kiss me already?"

"Absolutely, my darling." His arms came around her back, closing the final distance between them, and when his lips touched hers, there was a hint of something new in his kiss, a depth that hadn't been there before. She parted her lips and the kiss intensified, awakening wonderful stirrings within her.

Julie reciprocated what Max gave her and the emotion swelled in her heart as she put everything into the kiss, showing Max the way she felt about him.

She could hardly wait for the coming months as they had the chance to know more of each other and deepen their relationship, especially while being Max's girlfriend.

Life was very good after all.

Dear Reader,

Thank you so much for reading Prince Max and Julies's story, *Serving The Prince.* I hope you've enjoyed reading it as much as I enjoyed writing it.

Please consider leaving a review on Amazon and Goodreads. This is the best way to support me as an author.

For news of upcoming books and promotions, join my readers club at lucindawhitney.com.

I love to hear from readers! You can email me at lucinda@lucindawhitney.com.

Thank you!

About the Author

Lucinda Whitney was born and raised in Portugal, where she received a Master's degree from the University of Minho in Braga, in Portuguese/English teaching.

She lives in northern Utah with her husband and four children. When she's not reading and writing, she can be found with a pair of knitting needles, or tending her herb garden.

She's the author of the *Romano Family* series, and the co-author of the *Royal Secrets* series with Lindzee Armstrong and Laura D. Bastian.

Please visit her website at lucindawhitney.com for more information and news.